Franny in the Pumpkin Patch

By Siobhan Ciminera

Based on the television series *Franny's Feet*
created by Cathy Moss and Susin Nielsen

GROSSET & DUNLAP

GROSSET & DUNLAP
Published by the Penguin Group
Penguin Group (USA) Inc., 375 Hudson Street, New York, New York 10014, USA
Penguin Group (Canada), 90 Eglinton Avenue East, Suite 700, Toronto, Ontario M4P 2Y3, Canada
(a division of Pearson Penguin Canada Inc.)
Penguin Books Ltd., 80 Strand, London WC2R 0RL, England
Penguin Group Ireland, 25 St. Stephen's Green, Dublin 2, Ireland
(a division of Penguin Books Ltd.)
Penguin Group (Australia), 250 Camberwell Road, Camberwell, Victoria 3124, Australia
(a division of Pearson Australia Group Pty. Ltd.)
Penguin Books India Pvt. Ltd., 11 Community Centre, Panchsheel Park, New Delhi—110 017, India
Penguin Group (NZ), 67 Apollo Drive, Rosedale, North Shore 0632, New Zealand
(a division of Pearson New Zealand Ltd.)
Penguin Books (South Africa) (Pty.) Ltd., 24 Sturdee Avenue,
Rosebank, Johannesburg 2196, South Africa

Penguin Books Ltd., Registered Offices:
80 Strand, London WC2R 0RL, England

Library of Congress Cataloging-in-Publication Data

Ciminera, Siobhan.
Franny in the pumpkin patch / by Siobhan Ciminera.
    p. cm.
"Franny's feet."
ISBN 978-0-448-44836-7 (pbk.)
I. Franny's feet (Television program) II. Title.
PZ7.C4917Fr 2008

ISBN 978-0-448-44836-7   10 9 8 7 6 5 4 3 2 1

Franny Fantootsie loves to go to her grandfather's
shoe repair shop. She always meets new people
and goes on *frantastic* adventures.

"Those wings look heavenly," Grandpa told Franny as he fixed her costume. "You look beautiful, like a real fairy princess."

"But Grandpa!" said Franny, frowning. "The wings are crooked and the crown keeps slipping down. I'll never win the prize for best costume at the Halloween party."

Just then, the bell on the shop door rang and a man walked inside.

"A customer!" Franny cried.

"And what can we do for you on this fine day?" Grandpa asked the man.

"I can grow everything on my farm except new soles for these worn-out work boots," explained the customer.

"Don't worry," Grandpa told his customer. "We'll have these boots blooming again in no time. Franny, can you plant these boots in the fix-it box?" he asked.

"Okey dokey, Grandpa," answered Franny.

Franny walked to the fix-it box and set the work boots
down on the floor. She slipped her feet inside them.
"Where will my feet take me today?" she asked.
In a flash of stars, Franny was whisked to a faraway place.

Franny landed in the middle of a wonderful pumpkin patch. "Wowie!" Franny exclaimed when a huge pumpkin caught her eye. "That's the biggest pumpkin I've ever seen."

As Franny walked over to the pumpkin, it started to rock back and forth. "And it's dancing!" Franny cried.

Just then, a girl popped out from behind the pumpkin. "It's not dancing! I'm pushing it," she giggled. "Is it really the biggest pumpkin you've ever seen?"

"*Abso-franny-lutely!*" Franny replied.

"I knew it! My name is Ginny," she said, pointing to the pumpkin. "And this is Georgie the Giant. I'm entering him in the pumpkin contest at the fall fair! And I'm going to win!"

"I'm Franny. Nice to meet you, Ginny and Georgie," she said.

"There's one problem, though," Ginny began. "Georgie's too heavy for me to push to the fairgrounds all by myself."

"I'd be happy to help," said Franny. "And I'd love to go to the fall fair. We can push Georgie together."

Franny and Ginny stood behind Georgie. "One, two, three . . . push!" said Franny.

Franny and Ginny didn't get far before they had to stop. "Jeepers! Georgie the Giant sure is heavy!" Franny exclaimed. Then Franny noticed a wagon up ahead. "I've got an idea. Why push Georgie when we can pull him?"

Franny and Ginny rolled Georgie into the wagon—he was a perfect fit.

"Let's go!" said Franny.

When the girls arrived at the fair, Franny couldn't believe her eyes. "What a *frantabulous* fair!" she cried. "There's a pony ride, a Ferris wheel, and even a clown show."

"Come on, Franny," said Ginny. "There's no time for any of those things. We're here to win a contest!"

"I knew it! Georgie's the biggest!" exclaimed Ginny as she and Franny looked at the other pumpkins. "I better get a sticker for Georgie so that he's officially entered."

Jeepers! thought Franny. *Ginny sure wants to win the contest.*

Ginny came back and stuck the entry sticker on Georgie.

"Let's explore the fair while we wait for the contest to start," suggested Franny.

"Uh . . . I'd rather not," said Ginny.

"But there's so much to see," said Franny. "Don't worry. We'll be back in time for the contest."

"Okay," said Ginny, but she didn't sound so sure.

During the girls' walk, a bright red ball landed at their feet.

"Where did this come from?" Franny wondered. She looked up and saw a clown doing tricks onstage. The clown waved at Franny.

"I think he wants me to help him do a trick," Franny told Ginny.

But Ginny didn't seem to care. "I should go check on Georgie. I'll meet you at the contest."

"Okay," said Franny.

The clown began to juggle all the balls. Then he juggled them right into the hat that he gave Franny.

"That's a *frantastic* trick, Mr. Clown," Franny said, giggling. "I wish I could stay, but I'd better go find Ginny."

"Has it started yet?" asked Franny when she arrived back at the Giant Pumpkin Contest.

But before Ginny could answer, the girls heard a rumbling sound. They turned around and saw a pumpkin even bigger than Georgie being wheeled to the contest.

"Oh, no!" exclaimed Ginny. "How can Georgie win now?"

"That must be the judge," said Franny, pointing to the man who was looking at all the pumpkins. He walked right up to someone else's pumpkin and stuck the first place ribbon on it.

Ginny was disappointed. "I guess Georgie the Giant isn't so gigantic after all," she said.

"I'm sorry," said Franny. "I know how much you wanted Georgie to win."

"Look!" Franny exclaimed. "A Pumpkin Decorating Contest. Are you thinking what I'm thinking, Ginny? Georgie didn't win the Giant Pumpkin Contest, but he can still win for best-decorated pumpkin!"

"Great idea, Franny!" said Ginny.

Franny and Ginny had so much fun decorating Georgie.
They dressed him up like a clown with a big smile and a red
nose.

"How does Georgie look?" asked Ginny.

"He looks *frantabulous*—just like a real clown," said Franny.

Franny and Ginny watched as the judge looked at all the pumpkins.

"Oooh, I sure hope Georgie wins," said Ginny.

But instead of picking Georgie, the judge stuck the first place ribbon on a pumpkin that was decorated as a pirate.

"Sour pickles!" exclaimed Franny.

"I'm sorry," said Franny. "I was sure Georgie would win."

"Don't feel bad," said Ginny. "I don't mind."

"But I thought you wanted to win more than anything," said Franny.

"I did. But I'm having so much fun it doesn't matter," said Ginny. Then she took Franny's hand. "Come on! Let's go on a pony ride."

Franny beamed. "Okey dokey!"

Franny loved riding ponies. She rode a pretty brown pony and Ginny rode a pretty gray one.

"Let's go on the Ferris wheel next!" said Ginny as their pony rides came to an end.

"I'd love to," said Franny, "but I have to get home."
"But there's so much more to do!" exclaimed Ginny.
"I know, and you should do it all!" said Franny. "You deserve first prize for sharing such a fun day with me. But I really have to go."

"Bye, Franny!" said Ginny, waving to her new friend. "Thanks for everything."

"Bye, Ginny!" said Franny. "Have fun!" And with that, Franny was swept up in a cloud of stars.

"That was *funneriffic*!" exclaimed Franny as she landed back in her grandfather's shoe repair shop. Franny jumped out of the boots. When she put them into the fix-it box, something fell out of one of them.

"A sticker!" said Franny. "Just like the one Ginny put on Georgie at the Giant Pumpkin Contest."

Franny walked over to her shoebox in which she kept all her very special things. "Now I have another treasure for my shoebox!" she said, smiling as she placed the sticker inside.

Franny grabbed her fairy wings and crown and walked
over to Grandpa. "Can you help me with my wings again?"
Franny asked. "I have to get ready for the Halloween party."

"Sure thing, Franny," said Grandpa. "So . . . do you like
your costume a little better now?"

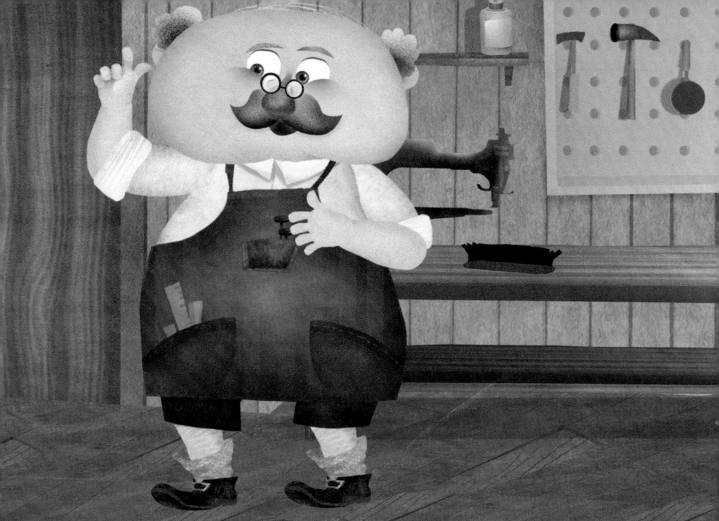

"Yes," answered Franny. "At first all I cared about was winning, just like Ginny. But now I know I'll have fun at the party even if I don't win the costume contest."

"That's very true," said Grandpa. "And as far as I'm concerned, you win first prize for being the best Franny ever."

"Thanks, Grandpa!" said Franny.

Franny went on a wonderful adventure today,
and another one is just around the corner. "Where
will my feet take me tomorrow?"